Gray Fox

By

Jonathan London

Illustrated by

Robert Sauber

Viking

VIKING
Published by the Penguin Group
Penguin Books USA Inc., 375 Hudson Street, New York, New York 10014, U.S.A.
Penguin Books Ltd, 27 Wrights Lane, London W8 5TZ, England
Penguin Books Australia Ltd, Ringwood, Victoria, Australia
Penguin Books Canada Ltd, 10 Alcorn Avenue, Toronto, Ontario, Canada M4V 3B2
Penguin Books (N.Z.) Ltd, 182–190 Wairau Road, Auckland 10, New Zealand

Penguin Books Ltd, Registered Offices: Harmondsworth, Middlesex, England

First published in 1993 by Viking, a division of Penguin Books USA Inc.

1   3   5   7   9   10   8   6   4   2

Text copyright © Jonathan London, 1993
Illustrations copyright © Robert Sauber, 1993
All rights reserved

Library of Congress Cataloging-in-Publication Data
London, Jonathan, 1947–
Gray Fox / Jonathan London; illustrated by Robert Sauber.   p.   cm.
Summary: Gray Fox is at one with nature and his place in it. When his
life is brought to a sudden end, we see—through the eyes of
a compassionate young boy—that nature offers recompense for loss.
I S B N 0 · 6 7 0 · 8 4 4 9 0 · X
[1. Foxes—Fiction.   2. Nature—Fiction.]
I. Sauber, Rob, ill.   II. Title.
PZ7.L8432Gr   1993   [E]—dc20   92-20653   CIP   AC
Printed in Hong Kong
Set in 15 point Goudy Catalog

For Sean and Aaron and my parents,
and for Joseph Bruchac.
—J.L.

⌘

To my father—along the
many paths I've encountered,
he's always shown me north.
—R.S.

Gray Fox runs
over rolling golden hills
in and out of forests
in the hot summer sun . . .
and laps cold spring water.

In the autumn
he tumbles among leaves
yellow-brown, red-brown, gold.

In the high woods
when winter comes
Gray Fox hunts rabbits—
tracks across the moonlit snow.

His fur grows thick
and he often goes hungry.

When he finds a vixen, a mate,
they make a den in a hollow
beneath the roots of a bay laurel.

Spring finds Gray Fox
and mate leaping through green
with their cubs, yapping for joy,
chasing butterflies,
learning to hunt,
pouncing in the wild mustard
flowering along the roadside.

One day, before dawn,
Gray Fox follows Rabbit
to the edge
of what he doesn't know about—

a rumbling thunder
of trucks and cars
double beams of light
barreling down in the night—

and decides to cross over.

Gray Fox—a silver sliver
of moonlight—*freezes*
in a speeding truck's lights

and the two tiny fires
of his eyes
flare up

and go out.

At the crack of dawn
a boy on a farm
finds Gray Fox
dead, in the middle of the road,
laid out across the center line.

He lifts up his still-warm body
not yet stiff—
his head and tail drooping,
his body bending toward Earth
as if he wanted to go back to it—
and carries him over to the side of the road.

No bones poke through.
His eyes are still open.
His ears are peaked like a puppy's
listening for a sound.
He looks alive, caught
in the middle of a leap.

The boy runs his fingers through
Gray Fox's bushy fur,
his neck and flanks the reddish gold
of his dad's beard.

Walking through dawn down River Road
the budding trees raising ghost arms
through the drifting mist

he carries Gray Fox as though
he were his baby brother.

He lumbers through fields with wild grass
and trees nearby
where vultures circle
high in the sky.

He goes to a place
down by the river
where no one goes.
Just he and the creatures
of the forest and river.
Where turtles sun themselves
on boulders, and osprey dive.
Where egrets step through shallows
and deer come down to drink,
and raccoons wash their food before eating.

He lays Gray Fox
in a bed of grass
where deer have slept.

As a jay squawks from a nearby tree
he kneels down and says a little prayer:

Gray Fox, may your spirit run free
may it do what it likes
may it find its new home.

"Goodbye, Fox," he says.

By late summer
Gray Fox's cubs
can catch their own meals:
grasshoppers, careless mice, floppy frogs.

Mother Fox grows content
watching her cubs grow big.

When winter comes
her cubs, fully grown now,
spread far and wide in their hunt
for mates—so they can start families
of their own.

By spring
Gray Fox's cubs
have cubs of their own:
like him
they seem to wear white bibs
and their necks and flanks
gleam with reddish gold fur.

And later, when they run
over rolling golden hills
in and out of forests
in the hot summer sun . . .

the spirit of Gray Fox
runs with them
like the wind.